"It was cool to have a crew to skate with, and I could imagine calling them friends. But not if I had to tell them the truth. Not if I had to tell them I was homeless."

DAX RAMIREZ
Age: 14
Hometown: Oakland, CA

STONE ARCH BOOKS
presents

written by

BRANDON TERRELL

images by

FERNANDO CANO AND LAURA RIVERA

a
CAPSTONE
production

Published by Stone Arch Books
A Capstone Imprint
1710 Roe Crest Drive, North Mankato, Minnesota 56003
www.capstonepub.com

Printed in Canada.
092013   007763FRSNS14

Library of Congress Cataloging-in-Publication Data is
available on the Library of Congress website.
Hardcover: 978-1-4342-3846-7
Paperback: 978-1-4342-6561-6

Summary: Skating at the local skatepark lets Dax Ramirez
escape from his worries of being homeless.

Designer: Bob Lentz
Creative Director: Heather Kindseth

Design Elements: Shutterstock.

CHAPTERS

SCAMMING

"All right, dude, time to pay up."

Fourteen-year-old Dax Ramirez kicked his battered skateboard up into his hand and tucked it under one arm. He waited patiently while the older kid next to him dug through the pockets of his baggy jeans and came out with a crumpled ten-dollar bill. The kid handed the cash over to Dax with a grumble.

"Hey, man," Dax said, shrugging his shoulders and cramming the money into his own pocket, "I beat you fair and square. Next time, try to actually land a kickflip."

"Whatever." The kid climbed on his board and pushed off, cursing at Dax but not looking back.

"*Adiós*," Dax called after the kid. Sometimes it was too easy. From the minute Dax had arrived at the skatepark that evening, he'd heard the kid bragging about his skills. So Dax had made him a friendly wager: ten bucks to whoever landed the best moves on the street course. Dax had won without breaking a sweat.

It wasn't the first time he'd scored cash at the park. There were always skaters who thought their moves could make them a few bucks. They were often wrong, and their money usually went to Dax.

Perfect timing, too, Dax thought. *I need to nosh.* As if on cue, his stomach rumbled.

"I hear ya, buddy," he said under his breath. He dropped his board and carved through the florescent-lit skatepark toward the concession area. A few skaters sat in metal booths eating junk food, and others stood alongside a nearby row of dented lockers. Dax spied the kid he'd just beat talking with his crew by the vending machines. When the kid saw him, Dax waved. The gesture was not returned.

"What can I get ya, Dax?" Andrew, the skatepark's owner, was manning the concession stand tonight. He was a young guy with a thick beard and wiry frame. He always wore a gray wool cap on his head, and the sleeves of his flannel shirt were rolled up, showing off numerous tattoos.

"Two of those." Dax nodded at the metal hot dog warmer and its continually spinning contents.

"Coming right up."

Dax took his dogs — all smothered in ketchup and mustard — and a bottle of soda to one of the booths. He ate alone, passing the time by sketching on his deck with a black Sharpie marker and by watching the other skaters stick moves off the park's halfpipe.

He was just polishing off the last bite when three kids about his age approached his booth.

"Yo, man," the tallest of the three said. "We heard you just hustled Will out of ten bucks."

"Yeah, I guess so," Dax said as he chewed.

"How are you on the vert ramp?" The tall guy grinned, an expression that spread wide across his face. "And do you have twenty bucks on you?"

Dax had played this game before. Having heard about the first wager, someone better came along and challenged him for more money. Some were good — and when they were, Dax left with empty pockets — but most of the time, they were all talk. Dax was confident enough with his skills to play those odds.

Dax nodded. "You're on."

The tall halfpipe had fifteen-foot transitions and steel coping. Dax started simple. He skated down the ramp and up the other side, pinning his deck against the coping with his front foot in a simple nose stall.

The tall kid — his name was Oscar — rocketed down the pipe beside Dax. He got air, then grabbed his deck with his back hand in an indy grab. It was a basic move, but Dax could tell by Oscar's fluid movements that the dude had skills.

Back and forth, the two dueling skaters showed off their best moves. Oscar would spin in a 360, and Dax would counter with a 540. Through it all, Oscar's friends cheered both of them on from the bottom of the pipe.

Finally, after Dax successfully landed a frontside invert,

imself too hard. He soared down the
the other side of the ramp, and flew into the air.
s deck in a 540 McTwist, but instead of the wheels
hit the ramp cleanly, his trucks connected with the coping
and he toppled into the pipe.

Oscar landed hard on the wooden ramp, striking his side
and knocking the air from his lungs. Dax watched from the
top of the ramp as Oscar staggered to his feet, cursed, and
kicked his board. It clattered end over end across the ramp.
Dax descended from the ramp to join him.

"You okay?" He nodded to the red bruise coloring one of
Oscar's forearms.

Oscar waved the arm a bit and winced. "Yeah, I'm good,"
he said.

A sharp whistle cut through the skatepark. Dax looked
over and saw Andrew, mop in hand, signaling the few
remaining skaters. They'd lost track of time, and Andrew was
getting ready to close up the park for the night.

"Here." Oscar handed Dax a twenty-dollar bill while one
of his pals recovered the errant skateboard. "You've got some
moves, man."

"Thanks," Dax said, slapping Oscar five. "You, too."

"All right, gang!" Andrew shouted. He waved his mop in the air. "Get out of here! Go on home, for crying out loud!"

Home, Dax thought. *Yeah. I wish.*

It was summer in Oakland, and as the sun set across the
bay it cast the city in brilliant shades of purple, orange, and
red. Dax wanted to stop, take the sketchpad out of his worn
backpack, and try to capture the beauty of it all. He was
running late, though, and his dad would be upset if he didn't
check into the shelter before nightfall.

Dax and his father had been living at Destiny House
for over a month. The place was a homeless shelter on
the east side of the city. His dad had lost his job working
construction, and finding a new job was proving difficult.
When they'd lost their apartment, they had been forced

to keep their belongings in their small car. For about a
week, they'd even had to sleep there. They sold the car
and bounced around from shelter to shelter for a couple of
weeks. Then a social worker told his father about Destiny
House. They'd been staying there ever since.

Dax crouched low on his deck, making a tight left turn
and running the fingers of his hand against the asphalt for
balance. Destiny House was halfway down the block, a plain
building with chipped paint and a faded green awning. A few
men and women wearing layers of clothes despite the warm
summer night stood outside.

Dax ollied onto the sidewalk, kicked up his board, and
walked through the building's glass double doors. Standing
behind a counter just inside the door was one of the shelter's
volunteers, an older lady named Helen. She smiled when she
saw him.

The lobby split in two directions. To the left was a large
space, as big as a gymnasium, where temporary residents
ate a warm meal and slept on cots for the night. There was
also a large common room with a television and a pool table.
To the right was a hall of rooms. These rooms were given to

residents who worked at the shelter as a way of earning a more permanent living situation. Dax went down this hall, to the last door on the right.

He could hear his father whistling before he even opened the door. Despite their situation, Luis Ramirez kept a positive attitude and a song in his heart. Dax wished he shared his dad's outlook.

"*Hola*, kiddo," his dad said as Dax entered.

The room was small. There was barely enough space for two metal cots, a dresser with a stack of books atop it, and a bathroom. His dad, a broad-shouldered man with a weathered face and a deep, gravelly voice, looked like a giant standing in the cramped room.

Luis was still wearing his Destiny House T-shirt and jeans, and he smelled like cleaning supplies. "Pretty messy dinner rush this evening," he said. "Where were you?"

"Out skating." Dax dropped his board on his bed and flopped down beside it. The cot's thin mattress was lumpy and uncomfortable, but it was better than sleeping on the street.

He reached beneath the mattress and pulled out a metal

lockbox. Then he counted all the money he'd scammed from skaters that day. Thirty-seven bucks.

"Here." Dax offered his dad the twenty had won off of Oscar.

Luis didn't take the bill. "Put your money away, son," he said. "Let me worry about providing for our family."

"Um, okay." Dax added the twenty back into his pile.

"Besides," his father continued. "Ms. Hubbell, the social services director at the shelter, lined up a job interview for me tomorrow morning."

"Cool," Dax said.

It was only the second interview his father had secured since living at Destiny House. Dax kept his fingers crossed that this one would be the one to get them out of this place and back into their own apartment.

While his father cleaned up in the bathroom, Dax unlocked the metal box and placed his new earnings in with the rest of his cash. It wasn't a lot, but summer was just getting started. He had a feeling he could scam quite a few more posers at the skatepark in the coming months.

After sliding the cash back under his mattress, Dax took

out his sketchpad. It was bent, torn, and nearly full. There were charcoal sketches of board designs and logos — some of which he'd copied with colored Sharpies onto the deck resting beside him.

Sometimes he used the sketchpad to draw skaters he'd watched at the skatepark. He tried to capture the action of launching off the vert ramp. He'd also taped photos or magazine clippings of cool graffiti into the sketchpad. He especially liked the work of Banksy, a mysterious British street artist and painter.

Dax used the back pages of the sketchpad as a journal. He'd been writing in it each night since they'd lost their home. His small, compact handwriting filled entire pages. It was the best way to vent about their situation. Plus it helped him stay sane, since Dax didn't own a cell phone and Destiny House only had one television.

Dax wrote until he heard his father exiting the bathroom. Then he clicked off the lamp beside his bed, casting his half of the room in shallow darkness. Dax hid the sketchpad under his pillow before his dad could see it, rolled over, and muttered, "G'night, Dad."

Luis — his hair wet, smelling of soap — plucked a book about positive thinking from a pile on the dresser. He lay down on his cot. It groaned under his weight. "Sleep well, son."

He wouldn't. Just another night at Destiny House.

The first thing Dax heard when he woke the next morning was the sound of his father humming. He pulled the scratchy blanket away from his face to see Luis standing before a long mirror that hung from the back of the door. He was dressed in a rumpled gray suit and was tightening his red tie.

When he saw Dax peering at him, he smiled. "Rise and shine, sleepyhead."

Dax groaned, then rolled out of his cot and staggered to the cramped bathroom to shower. After that he slid on the same Bones Brigade T-shirt and cargo shorts he'd worn the day before. When Dax rejoined his father, Luis was buttoning his suit coat and preparing to leave for his interview.

"Be good today," Luis said.

"Always."

"Wish me luck."

"Luck."

Luis flashed a nervous smile. Then he clapped Dax on the shoulder and exited the room.

It was late morning by the time Dax rolled up to the brick building that housed Wild Ride Skatepark. One of its walls had just been whitewashed to cover tags left by graffiti artists. Of course, it was only a matter of time before someone splashed new color on the empty, inviting canvas.

Behind the building was the park's outdoor course. It was already crowded with skaters. Dax could hear the clatter of their decks against concrete. Inside, the park was packed, too. Dax saw many of the same faces day to day, but there was also a steady stream of newbs who wandered from park to park. These were usually the ones who talked big and carried enough cash to make a friendly wager.

Dax snagged a helmet and pads from the rental counter

and stashed his backpack in one of the banged-up lockers. Then he hit the outdoor course.

He found a fun box and rail where he could practice. Then he rode up the box, kicked his board up, and caught the rail with his back truck in a smith grind before dropping safely back to the cement. It felt good to land a move, hearing the metal trucks sing against the rail, feeling the deck bend beneath his feet.

After a while, Dax found his way to the vert ramp. There, a young kid talking trash bet him ten bucks he couldn't be out-maneuvered. Dax, who only had a ten on him, accepted the challenge.

Should be easy enough to double my money, thought Dax.

It was clear that Dax was the better skater, and the kid knew it. He was nervously executing moves and barely landing them. Then, just after Dax had completed a lein air — an ollie combined with a backside grab — and was coming down the transition, he heard a female voice yell, "Head's up!"

Dax had zero time to react as a deck collided with his own. His legs tangled, and he fell hard onto his back. His

helmet struck the transition. It made his ears ring, and he squeezed his eyes shut against the pain.

"Oh my gosh! Are you all right?"

Dax was furious. He'd never been taken out by another skater before. His head hurt, and his right leg throbbed.

Dax peeled open his eyes and found himself staring up at a skater girl about his age. She had golden brown hair that framed her face and piercing blue-gray eyes that looked down on him with concern.

"Here. Let me help you up." The girl slid her arm under his and assisted Dax to his feet. "Man, I am so sorry. Are you okay?"

Dax slipped out of her grip. "I'm fine." He bent his sore leg, testing it by placing all his weight on it. Then he snatched up his board.

The arrogant kid rode up to them with a smile of relief plastered on his face. "Dude! Pay up."

Dax shook his head. "No way. That's so not fair."

"Hey bro, a bet's a bet." The kid held out his hand. His buddies looked on from behind him.

"Here. Try buying a few skating lessons." Dax dug into

his pocket, took out his ten, and slapped it into the kid's waiting palm. The smug kid and his pals skated away.

The skater girl watched them go. "What was that all about?" she asked.

"Nothing." Dax turned and began to head toward the lockers.

The girl followed him. "My name's Lucy," she said. "Say, I know you're mad and all, but my crew and I are about to cut out and get something to eat. Will you at least let me buy you lunch to make up for it, dude?"

Dax stopped and turned back to her. He didn't have any close friends, and he wasn't looking to make any. But he'd just lost the only cash he had on him, and a free meal was a free meal.

He shrugged his shoulders. "Sure," he said. "Why not?"

Lucy's crew consisted of three other skaters: Seth, a loud dude with shaggy brown hair pulled under a wool cap; Rae, a girl whose scrawny arms and legs bore battle scars from years of skating; and Tran, a short boy who was a year younger than the others. They all wore high-end gear and came from an upper-class neighborhood called Rockridge. Dax felt totally out of his league.

They stopped at a Mexican restaurant known for its mammoth burritos. True to her word, Lucy paid for Dax's meal. When she told the clerk she wanted them 'to go', Dax shot her a look.

"We're taking them to our own little secret spot," she explained.

"Our 'Fortress of Skate-itude,'" Seth added. Tran and Rae, who were filling their soda cups from the fountain system, laughed.

Dax was annoyed. He'd hoped to eat lunch and ditch these guys, then head back to Wild Ride or something.

Lucy snatched the grease-stained paper bag holding his free meal from the clerk and said, "Follow me."

They rode through the city — weaving in and out of the streets, carving down the sidewalks and getting yelled at by pedestrians — until they reached the outskirts of the city. A construction site surrounded by a chain-link fence took up most of one block. A tall building stood unfinished, a combination of metal beams, brick walls, and boarded-up windows. In the building's shadow, away from the street and passersby, the kids found a gap in the fence. They squeezed through the gap, one by one. It was clear that Lucy and her friends had been here before.

As he stepped inside the skeleton of the unfinished construction, Dax realized that the building was supposed to be a hotel. "The owners must have gone bankrupt and abandoned the project," Lucy said.

"I found it about a month ago," Tran added. "Check it out." He pointed across the spacious lobby to a separate room. Inside was the groundwork for a recreational space, including an unfinished, kidney-shaped pool.

Dax's jaw dropped. *Okay, maybe these guys aren't so bad, after all.*

They ate lunch poolside, lying on their backs in the shade. Dax remained silent while they talked about the private school they attended and about friends who were jetting off on exotic summer vacations.

After lunch, Dax took a turn riding in the pool. He'd skated in bowls before, but riding in a cement pool changed a skater's timing completely. He dropped in, quickly gained speed, and executed a backside turn in the deep end of the pool. When he hit the shallow end again, he drove his trucks against the cement edge of the pool in a frontside grind. Then he dropped back into the pool, carved around, and successfully launched out.

The quartet of onlookers applauded.

"Wow," Lucy said. "Impressive."

"*Gracias*," Dax answered.

They skated for most of the afternoon, and as much as Dax hated to admit it, he was having a good time. Rae was the most adventurous skater of the group. She whipped her body around in midair like she was never coming down.

Seth was good, but his technique was stilted. Tran rode fast, but because of his speed, he had a hard time landing moves. And Lucy was a smooth, elegant skater. Pretty, too. Dax caught himself staring at her more and more as the day went on.

Finally, as the afternoon waned, Dax scooped up his backpack. "This has been real," he said. "But I gotta jet."

Lucy looked bummed. "Oh. Okay."

"What're your digits, Dax?" Seth asked. "I'll text you next time we're heading to Wild Ride."

"I . . . uh, I don't have a phone," Dax said.

Seth's jaw dropped. "What? You don't have a phone? Dude, that's crazy."

Dax struggled to think of a reason why he wouldn't own a cell phone. Preferably a reason that didn't have the word *poor* in it. "Well, it . . . dropped out of my pocket on the halfpipe. Crushed it under my deck."

"That sucks. I don't know what I'd do without this thing." Seth dug his own phone from his cargo shorts and, as a joke, kissed it. "I love you," he whispered to the phone.

"I guess we'll see you around then?" Lucy asked.

"Sure." Dax stepped on his board. "Thanks for lunch."

"No problem." Lucy smiled at him, and Dax's heart skipped a beat.

* * *

When Dax reached Destiny House, his father was in the common room watching baseball on the television with some of the other guests. The Oakland A's were playing the Seattle Mariners.

As Dax approached them, the group of quiet men let out a mighty cheer. Luis motioned for Dax to sit. "How was your day?" he asked. "Do anything exciting?"

Dax shrugged. "It was fine. How was the interview?"

"I have a very good feeling about it." Luis held up one massive hand to show that his fingers were crossed.

I hope you're right, Dax thought.

Dax stayed to watch the remainder of the game. The A's pulled out a close win, and Luis and the others cheered and high-fived one another.

Together, Dax and his dad walked back to their room. Luis quickly fell asleep, his breathing deep and even. Dax dug out his sketchpad and wrote in his journal until his eyes were bleary and he could barely keep them open anymore.

Lucy and her friends weren't at Wild Ride the following day, or the day after that. Dax kept searching for them. He was actually bummed each day when they didn't show up. It was probably for the best, though. Dax had gotten along fine with them, but he hated lying. And he was too embarrassed to tell them the truth.

A few days later, Dax was sitting in one of the skatepark's concession booths, taking a break and enjoying a slice of pizza for lunch. The park was unusually quiet. Dax was hunched over his sketchpad, drawing a new design featuring butterflies and skulls. His box of charcoal pencils lay open beside him.

He was so caught up in his work he didn't hear Andrew approaching.

"Whoa," the skatepark owner said. "That's amazing."

Dax was so startled he nearly dropped his pencil. He quickly placed both arms over the sketch so Andrew, who stood beside the table, could not see it.

"Sorry if I scared you." Andrew indicated to the empty booth seat. "You mind?"

Dax shook his head.

Andrew slid in next to him. "I've seen the designs on your deck. You draw all of those yourself?"

"Yeah," Dax answered.

"Cool. Are you planning on going to art school when you get older?"

Dax shrugged. He was too busy living day to day. He never even thought about the future. Right now, college was a long shot at best.

"Mind if I take a look?" Andrew nodded at the covered sketchpad. "I mean, it's cool if you don't want me to or anything."

"No, you can." Dax slid the sketchpad across the booth.

Andrew scooped it up and flipped through the pages. He nodded, complimented Dax on a few logo designs, and even recognized a charcoal sketch of himself grinding one of the skatepark's rails. "This is great stuff," he concluded.

"Thanks."

Andrew stood. "Say, I was thinking," he said. "You know the side of the building, the one that always gets tagged?"

Dax nodded.

"Why don't you come up with a design, a mural that you can paint on that wall? I've been thinking about switching up the park's logo and look, and that wall is prime real estate. Sound cool?"

Dax's heartbeat sped up. To display his art like that in front of anyone who passed the skatepark? That was beyond cool.

"Ye-yeah," he stammered. "It'd be an honor."

"I'll pay for the supplies, whatever grub you eat while you're working, and maybe a bit extra when the whole thing's done. Deal?"

Dax nodded. "Deal."

"Awesome." Andrew offered his hand, and the two shook.

Then the skatepark owner sauntered off toward the rental counter.

Dax was in shock. It was an amazing opportunity, and he couldn't wait to get started. He quickly flipped his sketchpad open to an empty page, snagged a charcoal pencil, and began to doodle.

"There he is!" Seth's loud voice rang out across the skatepark. Dax looked up to see the quartet of skaters heading toward him. Lucy was in the lead. She wore a bright T-shirt, a pair of cut-off shorts, and hot pink Chuck Taylors. Her deck was tucked under one arm.

"Hey, stranger," she said.

Dax waved, noticed his art supplies spread out on the booth, and quickly gathered them up. He slid the sketchpad and box containing his pencils into his backpack, then crammed the bag into the booth beside him.

"Did you miss me?" Lucy asked jokingly.

"No," Dax answered. "That free burrito, on the other hand . . ."

Lucy laughed and punched him lightly on the shoulder. They all dropped their packs on the table and in the booth seat across from Dax. Then Seth said, "Come on, Dax. How's about you show us some of your sick moves on the street course?"

With his adrenaline flowing, Dax stood and joined the others as they pushed off across the skatepark floor.

GETTING ACQUAINTED

They rode for most of the afternoon. Dax showed Seth how to smith grind by locking his tail and truck on the rail. It took Seth a while — and a number of falls — to execute the trick. When he finally nailed it, the loud teen took a melodramatic bow. Dax whistled loudly through his fingers, then looked for the others. Lucy and Rae were practicing blunts and stalls on a couple of nearby mini-ramps. And the speedy Tran rode up one side of a fun box and effortlessly kickflipped back down to the cement.

Dax had tried to fight it, but it was hard to deny: he was making friends.

As they skated, the group shared with Dax a bit about their lives. Lucy had a brother who was heading to college in Boston. Tran's dad was a successful lawyer. And Rae and Seth were actually cousins.

"How about you, Dax?" Lucy asked as she ollied up into a 5-0 grind on a low rail. "What's your family like?"

Before Dax realized what he was doing, he said, "Oh, you know. The norm. Only child. Boring mom and dad."

"Where do you go to school?" Seth asked.

"Uh, Greenvale Prep." *Why am I lying to them?*

"Nice. I know a dude who goes to Greenvale," the usually quiet Rae chimed in. "That's an expensive private school."

"What do your parents do for a living?" Seth asked.

"My mom's a doctor. Dad's in construction."

"Is he like an architect or something?" Tran asked.

"Or something."

"Do you live nearby?" Lucy asked.

"Kinda."

Dax couldn't take it anymore. He was flat-out lying to these guys because he was so ashamed of the truth. So he decided to get away from the group and their interrogation.

He skated over to a nearby bowl and practiced a few tricks there. Solo.

Dax had promised his father he would have dinner with him at the shelter, so when the group went back inside to hit the concession stand, Dax snatched his backpack out of the booth, zipped it up, and hoisted it onto his shoulder.

"Bailing on us again, Dax?" Lucy shook her head in mock disappointment. "I'm starting to think you don't like us."

If only that were true. "You guys coming back tomorrow?" he asked.

"First thing in the morning."

"Sounds good. See you then." He slapped each of them five, waved to Andrew at the rental counter, then skated his way out of Wild Ride.

As he passed by the skatepark's white wall, the giant blank canvas just waiting for him to showcase his artistic talent, Dax was once more filled with excitement. He couldn't wait to tell his dad all about it.

* * *

Dinner was spaghetti and meatballs, garlic bread, and canned vegetables, all served on plastic trays like the ones at school. The food wasn't great, but Dax inhaled it anyway as he eagerly told his dad about how he was going to paint a mural on the outside of the skatepark.

"That's fantastic," Luis said in a loud, booming voice. Then he added, "Can you believe it?! My son's an artist!" The men and women eating around them glanced over and smiled politely. Dax felt his cheeks flush from the attention.

Dax couldn't wait to start sketching out designs again. He walked quickly back to their room while Luis helped clean up the dinner rush. When he got to the room, he leaped onto his bed, unzipped his bag, and rummaged inside for his sketchpad and pencils.

But the sketchpad wasn't there.

That's weird, he thought.

Fear began to snake its way around his stomach and squeeze. He tipped the backpack upside down and shook it. All that fell out were a couple of skate magazines, an extra set of bearings, and the box of charcoal pencils.

"Where's my sketchpad?" His voice was a whisper. Panic spread through every vein in his body.

He looked again, as if the sketchpad would magically

reappear in his pack like a lame magician's trick. Then it hit him. When Lucy and her friends had shown up, Dax had crammed the sketchpad back into his bag.

But I didn't zip up my backpack until I left.

The book must have fallen out at the skatepark. That was the only rational explanation. He wanted to rush out immediately and retrieve it, but Wild Ride would be closed. He would have to wait until the morning.

Dax was on edge for the remainder of the night. As crazy as it sounded, losing his sketchpad was almost like losing a limb. It was his most cherished possession, and now it was just . . . gone.

It was long after dark by the time Luis strolled back into the room. He and some of the others had watched the baseball game again that evening. Dax lay in the dark, curled in a ball on his cot. Luis did his best to remain quiet as he prepared for bed. But it didn't matter; Dax wasn't asleep.

In fact, he barely slept a wink that night.

Dax crouched low on his deck and rocketed down the sidewalk. His wheels clattered rhythmically against the asphalt as he sped from Destiny House to Wild Ride. He wanted to get to the skatepark before it was too crowded. He'd convinced himself that Andrew or one of the other employees had found and recognized his sketchpad when they were closing up. But he wanted to be sure it was safe.

Just as he'd hoped, Wild Ride was still pretty quiet this early in the morning. Andrew wasn't there. One of the other employees, a tired-looking guy named Gus sat behind the rental counter, sipping from a giant mug of coffee. When Dax asked him about the sketchpad, Gus shook his head. "Haven't seen anything."

Next Dax searched around the booth where he and the others had slung their belongings. Nothing. He bent down to search under the booth. *Nada.*

As he stood back up, he looked over and saw Lucy and her friends walking through the door, laughing with one another.

In Seth's hand was Dax's sketchpad.

He was both relieved and horrified. So many of his personal thoughts were written in the back of the sketchpad. About losing his home. About living on the street and being excited about going to school because it meant he got a free meal to eat. All of the things he was too ashamed to tell anyone.

When Seth saw him standing beside the booth, he held up the sketchpad. "Yo, man, you missing something?"

Dax snatched the sketchpad from Seth's hand and shoved it into his backpack. "Thanks," he said quietly.

There was an awkward moment of silence before Seth said, "So why did you lie to us?"

Dax froze. His blood ran hot, and his cheeks flushed with anger. "What do you mean?"

"What do I mean? Dude, you told us you go to Greenvale, and that your mom's a doctor. Not that you and your dad live in a homeless shelter."

"You read my journal?" Dax asked through gritted teeth.

"Had to figure out who the thing belonged to, right?"

"This is my private property." Dax could feel his hands shaking. He clenched his board, felt the deck's coarse grip tape cut into his fingers.

Seth shook his head. "Man, you are such a liar."

Without thinking, Dax shoved his board hard into Seth's chest, knocking the teen off balance. Seth fell into Tran, and together, the two stumbled backward, falling to the floor. Dax ran for the entrance. He could feel all of the other skatepark patrons staring at him, could hear Lucy crying out, "Dax! Wait!" and could feel hot tears forming at the corners of his eyes. But he didn't care. He was embarrassed and angry, and he needed to get away from it all.

Dax burst through the door, nearly knocking over a young kid entering the skatepark. He took off on his board.

He had no idea where he was going. He only knew that he didn't want to be seen at Wild Ride ever again.

* * *

Dax stopped in an alleyway a few blocks from Wild Ride and let the tears flow. Through everything he and his dad had endured, Dax had stayed strong. He'd never cried — not when they'd lost their house, not when they'd slept in their car, not even when they started staying at Destiny House. But now months of pent-up anger and fear came flowing out of him. He cried until his eyes stung and his nose ran and his chest heaved.

When he finally regained control of himself, he took a deep breath and wiped his nose on his sleeve. Then he stepped on his board again, and pushed off for nowhere in particular.

Skating calmed him, and the wind against his face helped clear his mind. He shouldn't have shoved Seth. The dude had a point. Dax had done nothing but lie to them. And why? Because he was ashamed? Because he wanted to impress them? Both? He needed to apologize. But he didn't think he could face those guys. Not yet.

Dax realized that he was only a block or two away from the abandoned hotel construction site. He cut across the intersection, ollied onto the sidewalk, and carved through an alley until he spied the skeletal structure. Then he ducked behind the building, found the gap in the fence, and snuck inside.

The empty pool was just what he needed. He quickly dropped in, gaining speed and momentum with frontside and backside turns. He didn't try any extreme tricks — mostly just 180s and the occasional stalefish grab — but it felt good to be alone with his deck.

When he needed a break from riding, Dax lay on his back at the bottom of the empty pool. He closed his eyes. It was so peaceful. He wished he could stay here forever.

His solitude didn't last long. Dax heard someone approaching, and for a brief moment, panic raced through him. Then he saw Lucy's head peer over the side of the pool.

"Hey. I come in peace."

She sat on the edge of the pool with her legs dangling over the side. She kicked them back and forth as if the pool were filled with water. "So, I get why you lied to us, Dax."

"You do?"

"Absolutely. It's okay to be unhappy about your situation. But you also gotta know, we don't care about that at all."

"Yeah, right. What about Seth?"

"Seth can be an insensitive jerk. But that's only because he likes you." She paused, and then she added, "We all do."

They sat together in silence for a moment. Dax didn't know what to say.

Finally Lucy stood. "Dax, where you live doesn't change who you are. In fact, you're probably stronger than anyone I've ever met." She stepped on her board. "See ya around. Hopefully."

She spun, pushed off, and rode away. Dax listened to the sound of her wheels on the cement growing quieter, quieter.

And then she was gone.

Dax could barely eat dinner that evening. Instead he just pushed his food around his plate a bit and hoped his dad didn't notice that he was sulking. He kept thinking about what Lucy had said, about how where you live doesn't change who you are.

He looked around Destiny House's dining space at the people seated with him. They were tired, beaten down. And yet many of them had smiles on their faces. They laughed and joked and ate together like they were family. They were thankful for a roof, a warm dinner, and a bed to sleep in. Dax hadn't noticed this before. He was so caught up in the fact that he was homeless to realize he was surrounded by people who were just happy to be with others.

Still, Dax needed a bit of fresh air. After dinner, he told his dad he was heading out for a bit to go skating.

"Don't be out late," Luis warned him.

"I won't."

Like before, Dax rode with no destination in mind. Whenever he saw a spot that looked good, he would stop and try a few tricks. He saw a low cement wall that was perfect for a backside 360 kickflip. He ollied up and locked into a frontside smith bump grind off a vacant bicycle rack. And when he reached a set of cement steps, he heelflipped into a tailslide shuvit out across the metal handrail.

It was well after dark by the time he stopped at a small, neon-lit convenience store to get something to drink. As he walked out of the store, he glanced down the block. He was close to Wild Ride and could even see the giant white side of the building from this distance.

By the soft blue glow of the moon, he noticed two figures standing by the wall. They were dressed in black, with hoods pulled up over their head. Dax had a sinking feeling in his stomach, and quickly rode off toward the skatepark to check it out.

Sure enough, as he got closer, he could hear the sound of laughter and the hiss of spray paint cans. The two shadowy figures were tagging the side of the skatepark with looping, colorful letters and symbols.

Dax rode faster. "Hey!" he shouted. "What do you think you're doing?! Knock it off!"

The two figures stopped and turned. Dax didn't recognize them. They were older than him. And by the looks of it, stronger, too. "Turn around and skate away, dude," one of the teens said.

Dax raised his hands. "Look, I don't want any trouble."

"Well, too bad, bro." The second teen, taller than the first by a good foot, dropped his can of spray paint. He lunged forward. Dax quickly turned. But his deck caught on a rock and wouldn't budge. He stumbled, stepped off his board. Right at the menacing teen.

The tall vandal shoved him in the chest, hard. The wind rushed from Dax's lungs, and he gasped for breath. His heels scraped against the curb, and he fell on his backside. His

elbows struck the asphalt, and shudders of pain vibrated up both arms. The two vandals had forgotten about the wall. They were focused on Dax. They advanced, towering over him. Dax had never felt so afraid in his whole life.

"Help!" Dax shouted, but there was no one on the street around them. "Someone help me!"

The back door to Wild Ride banged open, and suddenly Andrew was there. He was carrying two bulging garbage bags in his hands. Surprised, the two vandals whipped their heads around at the sound of the door. Dax quickly scrambled backward across the pavement, away from them.

"Hey!" Andrew shouted. "What's going on here?"

"Come on, let's go!" The two vandals took off, leaving their duffel bags and spray paint behind. They rounded the side of the building and disappeared down the street.

Andrew hastily chucked the garbage bags in a nearby dumpster and rushed over. "Dax? Is that you?"

Dax nodded. He was still lying on the cement, propped up on one bloodied elbow.

Andrew reached out a hand. "Come on, man," he said. "Let's get you inside."

A few scattered fluorescent lights cast a dim glow across the darkened Wild Ride, but the shadows and silence made the place downright eerie.

Andrew led Dax to one of the metal booths. While Dax sat, the skatepark owner rummaged around behind the counter. He came out with a small red first-aid kit and a roll of paper towels.

He pulled up a chair, set the kit on the table, and sat beside Dax. "Let me take a look."

Dax lifted his injured arm. Blood had dripped down his forearm. It was beginning to dry against his skin. Andrew silently examined the injury, then used a wet paper towel to wipe the blood and grit from Dax's arm. When the cold towel hit his scrape, fresh pain erupted in Dax's arm. He hissed through his teeth.

"Just a little road rash," Andrew said. "You're lucky, Dax. What did you think you were doing, taking on those guys?"

"I don't . . . I don't know. I saw what they were doing, and I just . . . got mad."

"Hey, man, I appreciate the concern, but the wall can be repainted. You?" He held up Dax's arm. "I can't just slap a coat of paint on this."

Instead he took a bandage from the kit and wrapped it around Dax's arm. When he was done, Dax tested it by bending his arm back and forth. "Thanks," he said.

"Sure." Andrew stood, putting away the unused bandages. "You should probably be getting back to the shelter now."

"Yeah . . . wait." Dax was floored. He'd never told Andrew a thing about his living situation. "How did you know I was . . . ?"

"Homeless? I'm perceptive, dude. I see you come in here every day, scamming money off kids because you need to buy lunch. I know how it is. I've been there."

"You've been homeless?"

Andrew nodded. "Yeah, when I was your age. Then I found a skatepark in San Diego that I loved, and a shelter for teens. I finished school and went to college on a scholarship. Through it all, my dream was to open a skatepark of my own, a place for others to feel . . . well, at home."

They were silent a moment. Dax could only spin one of the dirty composite wheels of his board.

"You're always welcome here, Dax," Andrew said. Then he rummaged in the pocket of his cargo shorts and withdrew a folded stack of cash. He counted out a few bills and handed them to Dax. "Why don't you stop by the hardware store tomorrow morning and pick up some paint," he instructed Dax. "I think it's time you got started on that mural. What do you think?"

Dax looked up at him and smiled. "I can't wait."

* * *

The next morning, Dax arrived at Wild Ride with two giant plastic bags filled with spray paint cans of every color. Andrew was waiting for him. A ladder leaned against the white wall.

In the light, Dax could see the incomplete tag started by the vandals the night before. It gave Dax an idea, and a wide smile crossed his face.

"It's all yours, sir," Andrew said, gesturing dramatically at the wall. Then he went inside and left Dax to work.

When the park opened, skaters began to trickle in. Many of them stopped by the wall to watch Dax and to ask questions. He met each of them with his own question, and all were quick to help him out.

Finally, as Dax was standing on the ladder, outlining what would become the centerpiece of the mural, he heard Lucy call out, "Well, what do we have here?"

Dax twisted on the ladder and looked down at the foursome. They all stared up at him quizzically.

"Hey, guys!" he said. "We're making a mural. Wanna help?"

Lucy dropped her board and rolled up the sleeves of her hoodie. "Where do we start?" she asked with a smile.

"Shhh! Everyone quiet! Here it comes!"

Dax cranked up the volume on the television in the community room of Destiny House as a commercial for a car dealership ended, and the music for channel 11's news kicked in. He sat back down beside his dad. On the other side of him, Lucy sat with a smile on her face while Rae, Tran, Seth, and Andrew stood behind them. The room was crowded with people, and Dax could barely contain his excitement.

"They say home is where the heart is," started the silver-haired news anchor, "and a local teenage boy is teaching a community that heart is all you need to feel at home."

When the news cut to various shots of Dax working on and standing beside the Wild Ride mural, the entire common room broke out into hoots and hollers. "That's my boy!" shouted Luis.

"Looking sick, dude!" Seth added, punching Dax lightly on the shoulder.

The shot panned across the entire mural. In the middle of the wall, Dax had painted two giant sideways skateboard decks. They were angled up and met at the tails so that they looked like an upside-down *V*. Beneath them were the skatepark's initials in blocky letters: WR. When seen together, the image looked like a house.

On every square space of white wall around the house logo were the tagged names of every skater who frequented Wild Ride. Their comments and designs turned the drab wall into a kaleidoscope of color.

The news story cut to a close-up of Dax. "This place is like a home to us," Dax said in the news story. "And I wanted to show everyone that home isn't a house. Home is all around you."

The story cut out to a wide shot of the skatepark. Dax,

Andrew, all of Dax's friends, and a large crowd of skaters stood next to the mural. They all waved at the camera.

When the news anchor started speaking about another story, Dax turned the volume down on the television.

"Man, that was so cool," Lucy said.

"Great work, dude," Tran said.

"Way to go," Rae added.

"All right, who wants a T-shirt?" Andrew reached into a giant cardboard box by the door and pulled out a shirt. He held it up, displaying the new house logo for Wild Ride. He tossed the first shirt to Dax, and Dax proudly slid it on over the shirt he was wearing. His friends quickly donned their own shirts.

"Is it okay if we go skating at Wild Ride for a bit?" Dax asked his dad.

"Go right ahead," Luis said with a smile. "I've got to get ready for my first day of work tomorrow."

"You certainly do," Andrew added. He wagged a finger at Luis.

Andrew had hired Dax's dad as a handyman to help out part-time around the skatepark. Granted, it was only until

Luis found a more permanent position elsewhere, but it was a start.

Dax and his quartet of friends skated to Wild Ride. As they carved around the corner next to the skatepark, Dax took in the mural again. It was so beautiful it took his breath away. He didn't think he'd ever get used to seeing it.

Dax's days scamming money off of other skaters were over; thanks to the mural, too many of the skaters now knew who he was and knew about his skating skills. It was cool, though. Dax didn't have time to make wagers at Wild Ride anymore.

He was too busy skating with his friends.

Dax and his dad continued to live at the shelter another six months, until Luis found a full-time, permanent position as a manager of an apartment complex. Dax works on his art and his skating daily.

L2S Solo

L2S Ramirez Hawk Face

L2S Wild Ride

SKATE CLINIC:
5-0 GRIND

1. Approach the obstacle in an ollie stance. You can either skate parallel with the obstacle or at a slight angle toward the obstacle.

2. Ollie up toward the obstacle. As you come down to land, push your front truck down and to the side of the obstacle. The nose should be below the edge as you start to grind.

3. When you land on the obstacle, most of your weight should be on the back truck, locking in the trucks so that your back wheel touches the obstacle. As you grind, make sure the pressure is on the truck and underside of the board.

4. When your front wheels are at the front of the obstacle, pop out of the grind.

SKATE CLINIC:
TERMS

5-0 grind
a move where a skater pops up onto an obstacle, then grinds his or her trucks along it

blunt
a move where a skater places the back wheels on the coping of the ramp and the tail is pressed against the ramp for a few moments

frontside invert
a move where a skater skates up the ramp and then does a handplant at the top of the ramp so he or she is balanced on the hand

heelflip
a move where the skater flips the board over with his or her feet

indy grab
a grab where the skater places his or her back hand on the toeside of the board

kickflip
a move where the skater pops the skateboard into the air and flicks it with the front foot to make it flip around in the air before the skater lands on the board again

McTwist
a move where the skater approaches the ramp wall riding forward, goes airborne, rotates 540 degrees in a backside direction while also doing a front flip, finishing in a forward position

ollie
a move where the skater pops the skateboard into the air with his or her feet

stalefish grab
an aerial move where the skater reaches his or her back arm behind his or her leg and grabs the middle of the board

tailside shuvit
a move where a skater slides the underside of the board's tail on a ledge, then spins the board under his or her feet 180 degrees before landing